A Great Idea

SCRATCHbot

by Adam Woog

NORWOOD HOUSE PRESS

Norwood House Press
PO Box 316598
Chicago, Illinois 60631

For information regarding Norwood House Press, please visit our Web site at:

www.norwoodhousepress.com or call 866-565-2900.

My thanks to Dr. Tony Prescott of the University of Sheffield,
England, for his time and patience. – A.W.

LIBRARY OF CONGRESS CATALOGING-IN-PUBLICATION DATA

Woog, Adam, 1953–
  A great idea : SCRATCHbot / Adam Woog.
    p. cm.
  Includes bibliographical references and index.
  Summary: "SCRATCHbot is a robot that depends on tactile touch to process
information. Using touch rather than vision, the SCRATCHbot aids scientists
researching animal behavior"—Provided by publisher.
  ISBN-13: 978-1-59953-380-3 (library edition : alk. paper)
  ISBN-10: 1-59953-380-4 (library edition : alk. paper)
1. Robots—Juvenile literature. 2. Tactile sensors—Juvenile literature.
3. Animal behavior—Research—Juvenile literature. I. Title.
  TJ213.5.W665 2010
  629.8'93—dc22
                                                              2010008502

Manufactured in the United States of America in North Mankato, Minnesota.
164N—072010

Contents

Note: Words that are **bolded** in the text are defined in the glossary on page 45.

Chapter 1

Meet the Robot Rat

Wild rats can be scary. They can even be dangerous, because once in a while they can carry diseases. But nothing is scary or dangerous about one special kind of rat. It is a robot rat.

This robot is called a SCRATCHbot. The SCRATCHbot is a cute little machine. It is bright yellow. It has a body, a neck, and a head. It moves around by itself on three wheels. A three-wheeled, bright yellow robot rat is pretty unusual, just by itself. However, this rat is even more unusual because it has no eyes. It is blind.

Using Its Whiskers

Being blind does not stop the SCRATCHbot from finding its way. This is because the machine has whiskers on the sides and front of its nose, like a real rat has. The whiskers can feel things that the robot finds as it moves, such as an obstacle.

The "head" of the SCRATCHbot is seen on the right. Stiff whiskers jut out from both sides.

The SCRATCHbot feels these things as it wiggles its whiskers. Its whiskers are sensitive and delicate. Like the whiskers of a real rat, they collect information about the position, shape, and texture of what they find.

Then this information goes to the computer "brain" of the rat. The computer uses this **tactile** information to instantly build a "mental map" of the space around it. Then the robot can move in the best way to get around any obstacles.

A Serious Purpose

The SCRATCHbot is a lot of fun to watch. It goes forward until it bumps into something. Then it backs up and moves around the obstacle.

But the robot also has a serious purpose. It is a scientific tool. The SCRATCHbot is important to science because it helps re-

Did You Know?

The SCRATCHbot's whiskers are 4 times as long as the whiskers of a real rat.

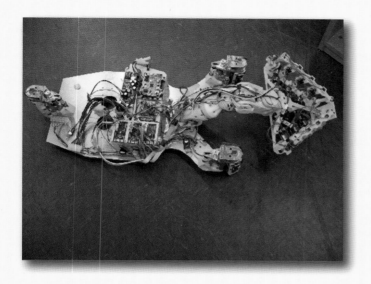

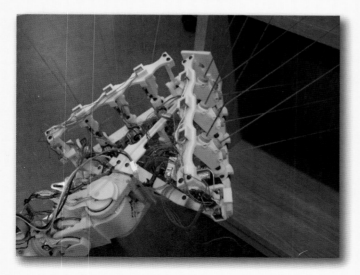

A SCRATCHbot is shown here in action. A close-up of the robot's head, below, shows its whiskers "feeling" a wooden shelf.

searchers study animals. These researchers need to find out more about how the brains of animals understand the sense of touch.

The lessons learned from building the SCRATCHbot are helping to make new and better robots. These new robots can use touch as their main sense for operating. Sometimes, only touch will work to direct a robot. For example, a robot cannot use vision when it is in a smoky room. So the SCRATCHbot is helping researchers build robots that can be used in more complex situations than other robots can.

What Robots Can Do Now

Many kinds of useful robots already exist. Most of them are used in **industry**. They

These large orange robots in an automobile plant are **welding** together parts of a car. The SCRATCHbot is able to perform even more delicate tasks.

are often better at some jobs than humans could be.

This is because these robots can do the same task over and over without getting tired. So they are used for boring jobs, such as putting together parts in a factory. Or they can do dangerous jobs, such as pouring molten steel, which is metal made liquid by heat.

Once these machines are programmed, they work almost completely by themselves. They do not need much human direction. That means that human workers can do other jobs that are less boring or dangerous.

One Problem with Robots

Researchers are finding even more ways to use robots all the time. But building better robots takes time. One of the biggest

No Need for Skin to Touch

People use their skin to touch things. The skin can tell if something is rough or smooth, hot or cold, moving or still. But animals like rats can do this even if their skin is not touching anything. They can use their whiskers.

The "whiskers" of a SCRATCHbot are much stiffer and less sensitive than those of this rat.

A Robot Taster

Touch is not the only sense that researchers want to give to robots. One team in Japan has made a robot that can taste things. It does this in order to check out what chemicals are in food and drinks.

By firing a special beam of light at the glass of liquid near it, this robot is able to "taste" and identify the liquid it holds.

problems is to find the best way for robots to recognize what is around them.

Right now, most robots rely on **visual** clues. For example, very strong robots are often used in buildings where newspapers are printed. These robots carry heavy rolls of paper from place to place. They are usually guided by tracks on the floor. The robots move by using lasers that "see" these tracks.

Some robots use video cameras, not lasers, to get their visual clues. For example, special robots can be used to investigate a bomb threat. A person stands at a safe distance and operates the robot by remote control. The robot's video camera lets the operator see where the robot is going, what is around it, and how it needs to move.

But vision is useless in some situations. For example, a video camera would not be helpful in a smoky building. Even if the robot used a bright light, it would not be able to see anything through the smoke. Many researchers feel that the best answer to this problem is to give robots the sense of touch.

One Solution to the Problem

Some robots already use a simple version of the sense of touch. They use it in addition to the visual information they get from video cameras. The development of these robots is an example of a branch of science called **bionics**. (Sometimes it is called biomimetics or biomechanics.)

In bionics, researchers study how living creatures do things. Then they build ma-

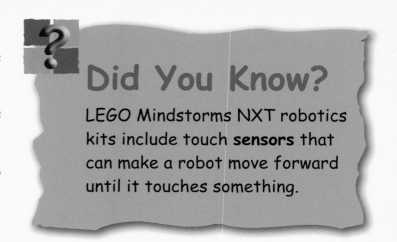

Did You Know?

LEGO Mindstorms NXT robotics kits include touch **sensors** that can make a robot move forward until it touches something.

chines that imitate those creatures. For example, bionics is used to make **artificial** parts for the human body, such as mechanical hearts and arms.

However, the design of robots that use touch is not yet highly developed. It needs to be studied more. The research team that is building the SCRATCHbot hopes to add to scientists' knowledge of touch-sensitive machinery.

A Sticky Invention

The science of bionics has been around for many years. What was most likely the first bionic invention became a familiar product. This is Velcro, which is used to fasten coats, shoes, and much more. It was invented in 1948 by George de Mestral, a Swiss chemist. He made it by studying the way thorns and other parts of plants stuck to his dog's coat.

Velcro fastens things by joining two strips of different material. One strip has tiny hooks, seen below, at right. These will firmly grasp tiny loops, seen at left and above right.

 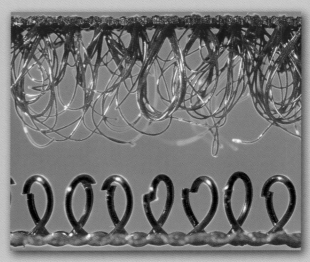

Chapter 2

An Idea Becomes a Robot

Two teams worked together to build the SCRATCHbot. Both teams are in England. One is the Active Touch Laboratory at the University of Sheffield. The other is the Bristol Robotics Laboratory in Bristol. The researchers who designed it are Dr. Tony Prescott, Dr. Tony Pipe, Dr. Martin Pearson, and Dr. Ben Mitchinson.

Their teams wanted to build a robot that imitated something in nature. They wanted this robot to imitate the way ani-mals use their sense of touch. When these teams began work on the problem of making a robot that relies on touch, they had to make many decisions. One impor-tant decision was to choose an example from nature that the team could use as a model for its research.

The researchers could choose from among many animals that use touch as one of their most important senses. For exam-ple, dogs and cats have sensitive whiskers.

Proudly watching a SCRATCHbot perform are three key members of the SCRATCHbot team: Doctors Tony Prescott, Ben Mitchinson, and Martin Pearson, left to right.

Touch is important to them. So are hearing and smell. This is because their eyesight is poor compared to their other senses.

Creatures with Whiskers

Many animals rely on touch even more than dogs and cats. For them, touch is their main sense. Some of these creatures are **nocturnal**, such as raccoons and badgers. Moles and other animals that live underground also rely heavily on touch.

Some sea animals, including sea lions, rely on touch as well. This is because they spend a lot of time deep in the dimly lit ocean. The sea creature with the most sensitive touch is a mammal called a **manatee**. It has sensitive hairs all over its body. Scientists think that these hairs are so sensitive that manatees can detect very small changes in the ocean's tides.

The SCRATCHbot team considered many animals when they were choosing one to study. The researchers decided to focus on rodents and **shrews**. Among the many kinds of rodents are rats, squirrels, and mice. These creatures really need their whiskers. Without them animals like rats

A manatee's whiskers are clearly visible on its snout. The creature also has hairs covering its entire body that make it very aware of its environment.

Touch-Sensitive Feathers

Many animals are sensitive to touch using their skin or whiskers. But not all animals use these to feel things. For example, many birds have tiny, sensitive feathers in addition to their regular feathers. These small feathers can detect tiny changes in air currents.

—and shrews—would have a very hard time finding food, noticing enemies, or even balancing themselves.

Focusing on Two Little Animals

In particular, the researchers decided to study two kinds of creatures, the Norwegian rat and the Etruscan shrew. Norwegian

Did You Know?

Someday people may be able to use touch-sensitive technology to "feel" the texture of clothes before buying them on the Internet.

tific studies. Researchers already know a lot about them.

The Etruscan shrew is the smallest mammal in the world. From the tip of its nose to the end of its tail, it is only about 4 inches (100mm) long. Its brain is twenty thousand times smaller than the human brain. Their

Studying the Etruscan shrew appealed to the SCRATCHbot team. Because it is not a rodent, comparing it to the rat gave the team additional information.

rats and Etruscan shrews use their sense of touch a lot, mainly because their vision is very blurry.

The research team decided to study these two animals for several reasons. The team chose Norwegian rats (sometimes called brown rats) because they are the most common kind of rat in the world. For this reason, they are often used for scien-

whiskers are very long, and they use them to hunt insects. The SCRATCHbot team chose shrews because they are not rodents, but they still use their whiskers in a similar way. The researchers wanted to see what the similarities and differences are between how rats and shrews use their whiskers.

Signals from Whiskers

A rat has about thirty whiskers on each side of its face. The creature can move these whiskers like a broom back and forth very quickly. This "whisking" back and forth can be as fast as twelve times per second.

A rat's whiskers are divided into smaller groups. Each of these smaller groups can move independently. Rats can also change the speed and direction of their whiskers.

Touching things with their fast-moving whiskers helps rats get a mental image of their location.

This lets rats sense things very efficiently. The small group of whiskers closest to an object will move less, while those farther away make larger, sweeping movements. This increases a rat's chances of touching objects that are farther away. This, in turn, helps the rat pinpoint its own location.

In both Etruscan shrews and rats, when their whiskers sense information about something, the information is turned into electrical signals. These signals travel through the animal's nervous system and go to its brain. Each animal then uses the information to form a mental picture or map of its surroundings. Then it can tell its muscles which way to move.

All of this happens in a split second, so that the creatures can react very quickly. (This is true of all animals. Think of what happens if your hand touches something hot.) This speed is important to both rats and shrews, in case they need to escape quickly from an enemy.

Building the Whiskers

The SCRATCHbot team needed special equipment to study how rats use their whiskers. One of the important tools was a video camera that takes 250 **frames** per

Shown here is the very first version of the SCRATCHbot. The small motor on the right with its long white strand of plastic lets the device "sense" things around it.

second. This is about ten times faster than a standard video camera. The researchers needed to use a very fast camera so that they could study every tiny movement that the whiskers made. The researchers also used custom-made lights and mirrors. This let them take videos from different views at the same time. Looking at different views of the whiskers' movements helped the team see exactly what was happening.

Using the information they got from the film, the researchers were able to design and build a set of artificial whiskers. These whiskers look a little like real ones, although they are much stiffer than those of a real rat. They are made out of high-tech plastic.

The SCRATCHbot has nine whiskers attached to each side of its head, so the to-

Plastic Muscles

The SCRATCHbot will change a lot as its inventors find ways to make it better and more like a real rat. For example, the researchers are experimenting with replacing the motors that move the robot's whiskers with a special plastic that changes shape when activated by electricity. This plastic works more like the muscles of animals.

tal is eighteen. The whiskers are divided into groups of three. Each group has its own electric motor for whisking back and forth. Each individual whisker has a sensor at its tip that feels the surface of anything it touches.

The whiskers on the left and right sides can operate separately, depending on the situation. For example, as the robot goes through a tunnel, it might be closer to one side of the tunnel than the other. If the whiskers on the left side are closer to the wall, those on the right might not touch anything.

In that case, the whiskers on the left side will continue to follow the wall, moving at a normal speed. At the same time, the whiskers on the right side will move faster than the ones on the left side, trying to notice anything on that side and make contact with it.

On the left, a SCRATCHbot explores a box. Its head appears below. The robot's design is very complex, and researchers want to make even more improvements to the device.

The robot's artificial whiskers can reach pretty far, but they are much slower than a real rat's whiskers. The robot's can move only about five times per second.

Building the Rest of the Robot

While the research team was designing and building these whiskers, it was also creating the head, neck, and body of the robot.

In addition to the main whiskers on each side of its head, the SCRATCHbot also has small, short bristles on the front of its snout. These short bristles do not move, but they are sensitive to touch.

The neck of the SCRATCHbot can go up, sideways, and forward. This lets the robot move its head and whiskers around.

A Good Memory

Rats can remember what they learn by touching things with their whiskers. That way, the animals can easily travel the same paths over and over. The SCRATCHbot's inventors will soon be able to give the robot the same large amount of memory.

The robot has a bright yellow body. On this body is most of the computer gear that the robot needs. The body also has three wheels underneath. Each wheel has its own motor.

Moving

As they were designing the SCRATCHbot, the researchers wanted it to be able to sense things a real rat can sense. This was important because the team wanted to understand exactly how rats use whiskers. So the researchers gave the whiskers sensors on their tips, just like a real rat. When the robot is moving and the tip of one of its whiskers touches something, the sensor in the whisker "knows" it. The sensor converts the information to a pulse of electricity and sends it to the computer "brain" in the SCRATCHbot's body.

The computer then sends an electrical signal to the head of the robot, telling the robot how to move its head until the tiny whiskers on its snout touch the object. These whiskers give the robot even more information. This new information includes clues about details such as small shapes or faint textures.

When this information reaches its brain, the robot then knows enough that it can move its body. The computer brain sends signals to the motors that control the robot's wheels. The machine can then move without bumping hard into anything.

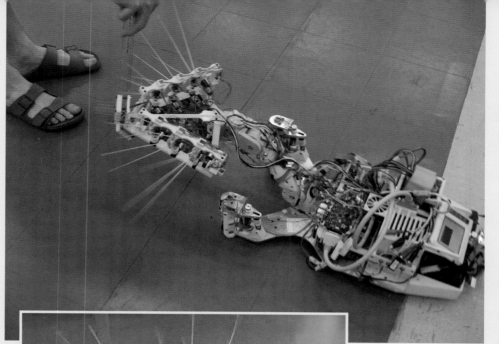

The technology that the SCRATCHbot team developed is the most important thing about the SCRATCHbot project. Of course, all of this research took a lot of work and study, but it was worth it. Scientists have learned a lot from creating touch-sensitive robots like the SCRATCHbot.

The SCRATCHbot itself is not the final product. Many more and better versions of it will be made in the future. However, the little robot has already been very useful. By studying rats and shrews,

The top photo shows a SCRATCHbot sensing a ruler. The robot moves its head, below, from side to side to sense things around it.

Scientists in Canada have developed a furry robot rabbit that uses touch-sensitive technology to respond to how it is petted. This "Haptic Creature" can respond by breathing, purring, or moving its floppy ears.

the SCRATCHbot team has added valuable information to an area of research that has a bright future. The discoveries they have made add to what scientists already know about how the natural world works. As researchers continue to study animals and insects, it is likely that more surprising technological discoveries will emerge.

Scientists and inventors are in the business of improving technology and other aspects of life. Sometimes, as with the SCRATCHbot, an invention opens doors that create amazing possibilities. The world can expect more exciting developments in the field of robotics.

Chapter 3

How the SCRATCHbot Can Help the World

Even before SCRATCHbot was completed, companies around the world were already finding practical ways to use different kinds of touch-sensitive robotic technology.

Some of these are just for fun. For example, several companies make touch-sensitive robot dogs and other "pets." Compared to real robots, these robot pets are very simple. Still, they are fun to play

Helicopters with Skin

Touch-sensitive technology is starting to be used in other ways besides building robots. One way will be to help prevent flying accidents. For example, helicopters could have touch-sensitive "skin" on their undersides. If the helicopter comes too close to the ground, the skin will warn the pilot.

The "Roomba," a robotic vacuum cleaner, is shown hard at work vacuuming a rug. Its sensors allow it to avoid obstacles.

with. They can follow a few commands or play music and move when someone touches them.

Other kinds of robots that are already available to buy are more useful. For example, a few companies make touch-sensitive robot floor cleaners. These robots can sense when they bump up against things. Among the machines that are already available are vacuum cleaners, floor washers, and pool cleaners. However, these robots are still in the early stages and will get more precise over time.

Search and Rescue

When touch-sensitive technology becomes more advanced, some robots that are now

Old-School Cleaning Robots

The idea of robot vacuum cleaners has existed for many years. In 1950 a science fiction writer, Ray Bradbury, wrote a story in which little cleaning robots tidy up a house.

This 1978 robot was designed to handle housekeeping chores. The designers even gave it a bow tie!

being developed will have important jobs. One of the most important of these jobs is to help during search-and-rescue missions. Search-and-rescue robots are already used to look for people who are trapped in dangerous situations. They are called Urban Search and Rescue (USAR) robots.

One of the USAR robots now being used is called the Packbot. It is used mainly by the military, doing jobs in dangerous areas. For example, it can disarm bombs while the operator stays a safe distance away.

This sturdy USAR robot is designed to work in places hit by earthquakes.

Soon, some USAR robots will be able to operate using only touch. However, right now they use video cameras as their main sense. Human operators guide USAR robots by remote control. The operator usually looks at a computer screen to see details about where the robot is going.

Earthquakes, Fires, and More

Touch-sensitive robots will be used for other important operations soon. A touch-sensitive robot in a situation such as an earthquake or

This USAR robot has cameras, gas sensors, and microphones to help locate people in risky places.

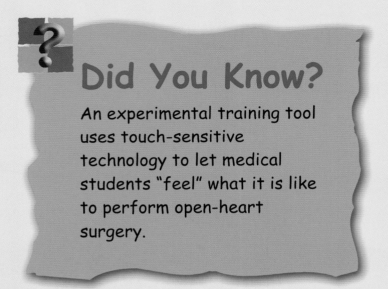

fire will locate people in two ways. One will be direct touch—that is, coming into contact with a trapped person. The robot will also have temperature sensors. These sensors will be able to feel the heat of a person's body.

After finding a person, the search robot will be able to radio its exact location to rescuers. This will cut down on the amount of time needed for the search. The faster a person is found in a dangerous situation, the better chance that person has for survival. In this way, touch-sensitive robots will be able to save lives.

Other Practical Uses

SCRATCHbot's technology continues to gain uses. For example, researchers are developing a waterproof touch-sensitive robot for exploring water that light cannot penetrate. Such places include the deep sea, underground tunnels, and tanks that are filled with dirty or dangerous liquids. This ability will let robots learn things when they are in places where "sighted" robots will not work. It will also be safer, since human divers will not have to go into dangerous places.

Touch-sensitive robots will also make medical treatment better. One example of this is a touch-sensitive robot being created by a Canadian research team. This robot will be able to quickly and accurately find cancer during an operation.

Right now, robots are sometimes used in surgery, but they are not touch-sensitive. For example, during an operation surgeons usually identify diseased **tissue** by feeling it directly. This is possible because diseased tissue and healthy tissue do not feel the same. Some diseased tissue is much harder than normal tissue.

But a robot that uses touch to sense this difference will be a big improvement. The robot will be able to find the diseased tissue more easily and accurately than human surgeons. The robot will be able to

do this because it will have a much more sensitive touch than the fingers of the surgeon. Also, the kinds of surgical robots that are already being used are very small. Surgeons have to make only very little cuts in the skin, usually less than 0.5 inch to 1 inch (1.27cm to 2.5cm) in length. One cut is for very small instruments, and the

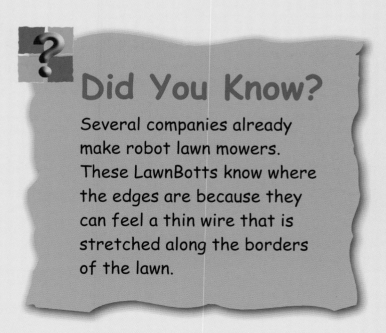

Did You Know?

Several companies already make robot lawn mowers. These LawnBotts know where the edges are because they can feel a thin wire that is stretched along the borders of the lawn.

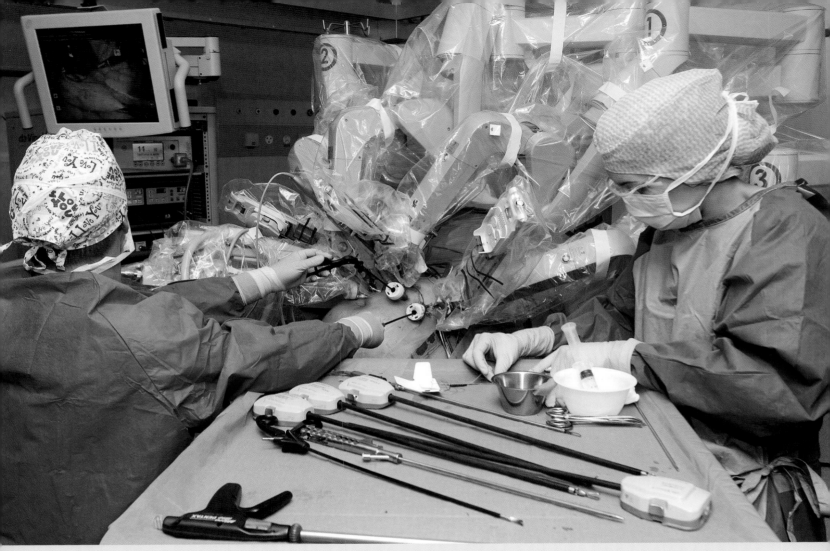

Doctors perform surgery using the robotic da Vinci Surgical System. Only a small surgical cut is needed—even for complicated operations. This means that patients heal more quickly.

other is for a tool that lets the surgeons see what they are doing. With such tiny cuts, patients have less pain and heal faster.

Touch-Sensitive Helper Robots and Artificial Limbs

Many other medical uses for touch-sensitive robots are being developed. For example, Japanese researchers are creating machines that will help elderly, sick, or disabled people.

The robots are being designed to help these people eat, lift things, and do other jobs. They will even help people get in and out of bed. These helper robots will need to be touch-sensitive, so that they can do their jobs without hurting the patient.

Soon, improvements in touch-sensitive technology will make artificial limbs even better. These new kinds of limbs will be able to transfer the sensation of touch directly back to the user's brain. The artificial hand or foot will do this by sending electrical signals directly to the user's

Touch-Sensitive Teddy

Many toys are touch-sensitive, such as dolls that laugh when they are touched. But even toys can have a serious purpose. A research team has created a teddy bear with two thousand touch sensors all over its body. It also has a speaker in its mouth and cameras in its eyes. It will help people who need companionship. It can also help children learn a language.

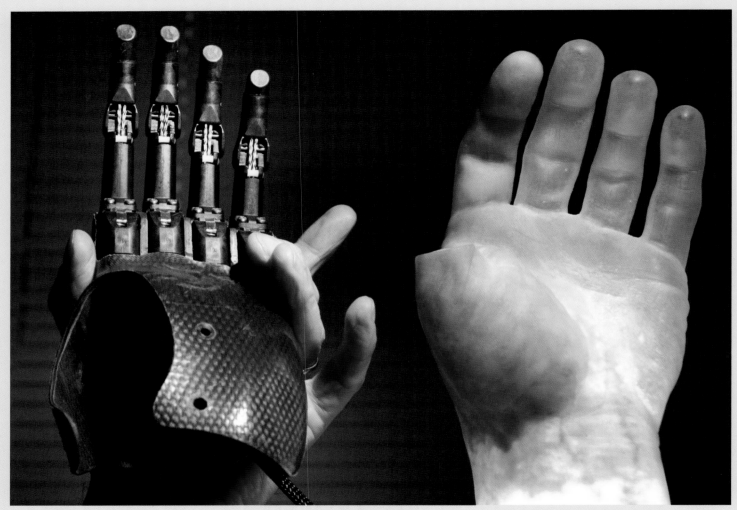

In December 2009, a Scottish company introduced the first bionic fingers, left, which can be covered with robotic skin, right—greatly improving the lives of people with missing fingers.

Did You Know?

A gaming company in America has developed a 3-D hand-control device that uses touch-sensitive technology to let users feel their way around obstacles in virtual space.

nervous system. To the person, it will feel like a real hand or foot.

Much More to Do

Many of these different types of touch-sensitive robotic devices are still in the early stages of development. They are not yet available to the public.

So a lot of work must still be completed before devices like the SCRATCHbot become really useful. However, the future holds great promise for touch-sensitive robotics. As part of improved technology in medicine, rescue operations, and other fields, they will be able to help make the world better.

Chapter 4

The SCRATCHbot Moves into the Future

Many things about touch-sensitive technology need improvement. A rat's sense of touch is very good at doing its task. So the team that created the SCRATCHbot is figuring out ways to make it perform more like a real rat. For one thing, the robot's body still moves much too

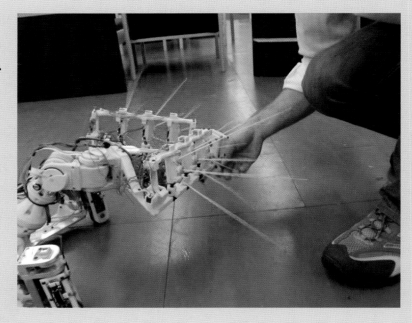

A SCRATCHbot uses its whiskers to detect a hand. The inventors are working to make its whiskers more like rat whiskers.

slowly. Its whiskers also move much more slowly than a real rat's whiskers.

Furthermore, the SCRATCHbot's whiskers are not nearly as sensitive to touch as those of a real rat. Nor are they as strong. Real rats can still use their whiskers even if they are damaged. However, the SCRATCHbot cannot work if its whiskers are damaged. The team is also figuring out how to make it easier to replace an artificial whisker if it does get damaged.

With whiskers that are faster, more sensitive to touch, and stronger, the robot rat will be much better. For example, it will be able to tell the difference between a smooth surface and a rough one. When it has more sensitive touch, the robot will be able to identify things more accurately. The robot will also be able to determine

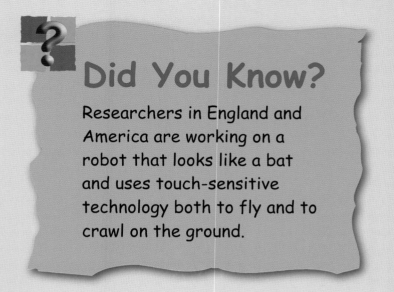

Did You Know?

Researchers in England and America are working on a robot that looks like a bat and uses touch-sensitive technology both to fly and to crawl on the ground.

whether a surface is curved or shaped in an unusual way. This ability will help it know how to make its next move.

The SCRATCHbot's computer brain also needs to be improved. It needs to become more powerful. Right now, it cannot store a lot of information about places it has already been.

The Touch-Sensitive Teaching Suit

Touch-sensitive technology may someday help people learn to move correctly. Researchers are developing a kind of "teaching suit." If the student makes a mistake, the suit gently vibrates. If the move is done correctly, there is no vibration. The suit could teach tennis players to play better, or it could teach people with brain damage how to walk again.

But having a bigger brain will let the robot build "maps" of its environment, just like a real rat. The robot's computer brain will store these maps. The maps will then let the device remember how to move when it encounters something it has felt before.

Moving Forward

One of the goals of the research teams developing touch-sensitive robots will be to figure out the best way for devices to communicate with people. A search-and-rescue robot, for instance, will need to send information back to a human operator somehow. This information will give precise instructions to the operator when the robot finds its target.

The technology that tells the SCRATCHbot how to travel also needs to be improved. For example, a touch-sensitive robot should be able to sense changes in the surfaces it goes over. This can be done with special sensors on the device's underside.

That way, the robot will precisely know whether it is on a soft surface, such as car-

pet, or a hard surface, such as a wooden floor. With this information, the device can automatically adapt to move ahead in the best way. This will be especially useful for machines like floor-cleaning robots.

Big Wheels? Legs?

The SCRATCHbot team and other researchers are also experimenting with different means of travel besides wheels. One possibility is to replace the wheels with legs. Other possibilities are oversize tires or treads like a tank.

Perhaps a combination of these will be best. With several choices, a robot

This rescue robot is being used to explore the rubble of a six-story building in Germany that collapsed in 2009.

Robots in Space

Vladimir Lumelsky is a scientist with the National Aeronautics and Space Administration (NASA). He is an expert on robots. He thinks that it will be important for robots to be touch-sensitive if they are used to explore other planets. Lumelsky comments, "Robots move well on their own, especially when nothing is in the way. Robots should be able to react [with touch], but today's robots can't. . . . That's got to change for exploration."

Source: *Robotorama*, "Robotic Skin," June 8, 2005. www.robotorama.com/page/3.

Shown here is an image of the Mars Exploration Rover *Spirit* as it appeared while exploring the planet Mars in 2004.

Did You Know?

Scientists are developing robot butlers and cooks that will use touch-sensitive technology to help out around the house. For example, they could stir a soup while a person adds ingredients.

searchers think will be possible. In that case, oversize tires might be better in sand, while legs would be better in rocky terrain.

Many of these alternative ways of movement for robots are already being tested now. Some of these machines have strange shapes. For example, a research lab in Japan is working on a robot that slithers on the ground like a snake.

Pure Science

As the SCRATCHbot improves, the information that scientists learn will help develop more and more new and useful robots. But, as the research continues, it will also uncover new information in pure science. Pure science is research that is focused only on discovering knowledge.

could switch from one to another as it needed to. Robots like the SCRATCHbot will then be more adaptable to changes in the surface of floors or ground. They will be able to travel easily even if these surfaces are very uneven.

Suppose a robot is exploring the surface of another planet, as some re-

Dr. Tony Prescott, one of SCRATCHbot's developers, is clearly delighted with the whiskered invention. Its vivid color is as bright as its future.

It does not focus on finding practical uses for what it discovers.

In fact, Dr. Prescott says that the SCRATCHbot team is mostly interested in pure science. He feels that it will probably be up to other researchers to create practical uses for touch-sensitive robots.

One of the main areas of pure science that the team is studying has to do with the biology of animals. They want to know exactly how animals sense touch, receive information about it in the brain, and then use it. These discoveries will add to the amount of knowledge scientists have about life on this planet.

Touching a Coin

Researchers around the world are developing many kinds of touch-sensitive technology. For example, a team at the University of Nebraska is developing an ultrathin, touch-sensitive artificial skin. It is made from very thin layers of gold and a metal called cadmium. The film is so sensitive that it can feel changes in a surface as tiny as the lettering on a coin.

This man's hand was badly burned in a house fire. He now has artificial skin on his hand and hopes to regain full use of his hand after healing and therapy.

Did You Know?

Touch-sensitive robots might someday be used to capture insect pests. They would imitate the way a shrew uses its whiskers to find insects to eat.

The SCRATCHbot team and other researchers believe that one important way to learn more about the biology of animals is by building robots that imitate them. This will make a positive contribution to understanding biology.

Of course, no one knows just what will happen in the future, with the SCRATCHbot or any other kind of touch-sensitive robot. But there seems to be little doubt that the device, and other robots like it around the world, will help make the world a better place. That is quite an achievement for a cute yellow robot rat.

Glossary

artificial: Something that is not natural.

bionics: The science of building machines that imitate things in nature. Bionics is sometimes called biomimetics or biomechanics.

frames: The still images in movies or videos that give the feeling of movement when they are seen one after the other very quickly. Film and video cameras usually take twenty-four frames per second.

industry: Businesses that manufacture or create things.

manatee: A large sea mammal, sometimes called a sea cow.

nocturnal: Awake and active at night. Nocturnal animals include bats, raccoons, and owls.

sensors: Devices that sense something and send the information somewhere, usually by electricity.

shrews: Tiny animals that look like mice. Shrews have whiskers like rodents, but they are not rodents.

tactile: Having to do with touch.

tissue: A group of living cells. Organs and skin are made of tissue.

visual: Having to do with sight.

welding: To join pieces of metal by heating. When the molten metal cools, the pieces bond firmly together.

For More Information

Books

David Astolfo, Stephen Cavers, Kevin Clague, and CS Soh, *10 Cool LEGO Mindstorms: Dark Side Robots, Transports, and Creatures*. Burlington, MA: Syngress, 2002. This book has instructions for building robots using LEGO Mindstorms.

Barbara J. Davis, *The Kids' Guide to Robots*. Mankato, MN: Capstone, 2009. A good introduction for young readers to the world of robots.

Adam Woog, *The Bionic Hand*. Chicago: Norwood House, 2010. This book explores the development of a new type of artificial hand.

Web Sites to Visit

NOVA Online: Bomb Squad: Hazardous Duty Robots (www.pbs.org). PBS offers this Web site, which includes a game to match the correct robot to three dangerous situations.

Robotics (www.thetech.org). This Web site is maintained by the Tech Museum of Innovation. It has some great pictures and information about robots.

Robots with Whiskers (www.brl.ac.uk). This Web site, maintained by the British Robotics Laboratory, has a short video of the SCRATCHbot in action.

Index

Picture Credits

Cover photo: Bristol Robotics Laboratory, UK
AP Images, 29, 32, 34, 40
Bristol Robotics Laboratory, UK, 5, 7 (both photos), 9, 14, 16, 17, 18, 20 (both photos), 23 (both photos), 36, 42
© Robert Canis/Alamy, 12 (both photos)
The Commercial Appeal/Landov, 43

David Elkins/*Midland Daily News*/AP Images, 26
Douglas Faulkner/Photo Researchers, Inc., 15
Getty Images, 39
© Christopher Honeywell/Alamy, 8
Hulton Archive/Getty Images, 27
Shizuo Kambayashi/AP images, 10
Katsumi Kasahara/AP Images, 28

About the Author

Adam Woog has written many books for adults, young adults, and children. He also writes a monthly column about books for the *Seattle Times*. Woog lives with his wife in Seattle, Washington. They have a college-age daughter.